LOST
ON A MOUNTAIN
IN MAINE

"I started to run and found I couldn't, because of the boulders; that made me frantic and I climbed over them like a cat and yelled and shouted and cried all the time. I yelled for my Dad. I climbed up as high as I could on a big rock and screamed for him—then I waited. No answering shout—nothing—just the noise of that wind and the purring sound of fine sleet driving against my clothes."

LOST
ON A MOUNTAIN
IN MAINE

by Donn Fendler as told to Joseph B. Egan

A Beech Tree Paperback Book
NEW YORK

Printed in the United States of America
First Beech Tree edition, 1992.

10 9 8 7 6 5 4 3

Library of Congress Cataloging-in-Publication Data

Fendler, Donn, 1927?-
    [Donn Fendler, lost on a mountain in Maine]
    Lost on a mountain in Maine : a brave boy's true story of his nine
-day adventure alone in the Mount Katahdin wilderness / Donn
Fendler, as told to Joseph B. Egan.
        p.   cm.
    Originally published by New Hampshire Pub. Co, Somersworth, New
Hampshire, c1978 under title: Donn Fendler, lost on a mountain in
Maine.
    Summary: A twelve-year-old describes his nine-day struggles to
survive after being separated from his companions in the mountains
of Maine in 1939.
    1. Katahdin, Mount (Me.)—Juvenile literature. 2. Fendler, Donn,
1927?- —Juvenile literature. 3. Rye (N.Y.)—Biography—Juvenile
literature. [1. Survival. 2. Fendler, Donn. 1927?] I. Egan,
Joseph B. (Joseph Burke), b. 1879. II. Title.
[F27.P5F45 1992]
974.1'25—dc20   ISBN 0-688-11573-X   92-3250
                                                     CIP   AC

Contents

CHAPTER I

MY ADVENTURE BEGINS · *First Day*

THE TOP of Katahdin was just ahead. We could see it through a break in the cold, misty clouds that whirled about us. Henry wanted to race for it, but I shook my head. Those last hundred yards were heavy ones and, in spite of the stiff, rocky climb, I was cold and shivery.

Just as we reached the summit, the mist closed in around us and shut off our view of the mountain below. I was disappointed. Who wouldn't be, after such a climb? We waited, shivering in the icy blasts that swept around us, for another break in the clouds. Dimly, just like a ghost, we saw a man standing over to the right, on a spur leading to what is called the *Knife Edge. He saw us, too, and waved to us, then started towards us.

*The man the boys saw was the Rev. Charles Austin, Church of All Nations, New York City. The Knife Edge, along the sides of which dangerously sheer drops of 1,500 feet are not uncommon, is a curving granite wall, connecting Baxter Peak and Pamola.

Henry is the son of a guide and he seemed pleased. "Let's wait here until he comes over," he said, "then we can start back together—that's the best thing to do."

But I was cold and shivery. I never was good at standing cold, anyway. Nights, when Ryan and Tom slept with only a sheet over them, Dad always came in with a blanket for me. I thought of that, and of Dad somewhere back on the trail behind us.*

"Let's get out of here now," I said. I remember that my teeth were chattering as I said it, but Henry shook his head. He wanted to wait for the man.

I think Henry was just a little bit nervous and who wouldn't be, with all that big cloud-covered mountain below us and clouds rolling like smoke around us? But Henry was wise. I can see that now. He *knew* Katahdin.

I was nervous, too, and maybe that is why I decided to go right back and join Dad and the boys. Maybe I was sorry that I had gone on ahead of them. Maybe *that* had been a foolish thing to do. Such thoughts run through a fellow's head at a time like that. Anyway, they ran through mine and made me more and more anxious to get back to the folks below.

Donn's party—including his father, his two brothers, Tom and Ryan, Henry Condon and Fred Eaton—left the Katahdin Stream campsite on the Millinocket-Greenville tote road about one o'clock in the afternoon of Monday, July 17, to make the Hunt Trail climb. See map.

I had on a sweatshirt under my fleece-lined jacket. When I made up my mind to start back, I peeled off the jacket and gave the sweatshirt to Henry. "That'll keep you warm while you're waiting," I said, "But I'm going *back, right now*. I'll tell Dad you and the man are coming down soon."

Henry said I was foolish and tried to stop me, but I knew I was all right. I guess I thought I knew more than he did, for I only shrugged my shoulders and laughed at him. Just then, an extra heavy cloud rolled in around us. I thought of people being lost in clouds and getting off the trail—and maybe that hurried me a little as I pulled up my fleece-lined reefer about my neck and started down. Boy, I can see now what a mistake *that* was! A fellow is just plain dumb who laughs at people who know more than he does.

The clouds were like gray smoke and shut Henry from me before I had gone a dozen yards. The going was very rough, and the trail wound in and around huge rocks. It hadn't seemed so awfully rough on the way up—I mean the last hundred yards, but *then* you climbed slowly—while going down, you could make better time. I hadn't gone far before I noticed that the trail led me up to rocks that I had to climb over like a squirrel. That seemed funny to me, but I went on just the same, because a fellow forgets easily, and I figured going down was different, anyway.

MY ADVENTURE BEGINS

Nobody can really understand how rough the going is, up there, until he has tried that Hunt Trail in a mist. I suppose Henry would laugh at me for saying so. He's been over the trail so often. However, I wasn't worried—not just then. I kept looking ahead, expecting to see Dad and the boys break through the cloud at any moment.

Everything looks different in the clouds. You think you see a man and he turns out to be only a rock. It kind of scares a fellow, especially when you are alone and awfully cold.

When I had gone quite a distance over the rocks—far enough, I thought, to be down on the plateau—I stopped and looked around. I couldn't see anything that looked like a trail. I couldn't find a single spot of white paint.* I thought I *must* be down on the plateau, but could not be sure. There are plenty of huge rocks on the plateau, but the trail winds in and out around them. The going is fairly level and the rocks don't bother as long as you are on the trail, but *I* was in the middle of the worst mess of rocks you can imagine. I began to worry a little. Boy, it's no fun getting off the trail, when the cloud is so thick you can't see a dozen yards ahead!

One thing helped me not to worry too much.

---

*In hiking language, a "trail" does not necessarily mean a path. The Hunt Trail, for instance, is marked by daubs of white paint on trees and rocks. Where the markings take the form of arrows, their tips point in the direction of the summit of Mt. Katahdin, Baxter Peak.

I knew that if Dad and the boys were still on the way up they must be nearing the place where I stood. At least they must be within hearing distance. I shouted several times. Not a sound answered me. My voice seemed hollow. I had a feeling it didn't go far through that heavy cloud. I waited and then I shouted again and again. At last, I just stood and listened for a long time. No answering shout— nothing but the noise of the wind among the rocks. Boy, I felt funny when I started on.

I couldn't see far on any side of me and I had a feeling I was right on the edge of a great cliff.* The way the clouds swirled scared me. The rocks about me looked more like ghosts than rocks, until I tried to climb over them. Besides, sleet was beginning to fall. It formed slick, thin ice on the sleeves of my reefer, and I had to wipe it off my face. I didn't like that. I was wearing a pair of blue dungarees and I could feel the water seeping through and getting cold about my legs.

"Maybe," I thought, "I ought to sit down and wait for Henry and the man. They'd be along now any moment." But when I stood still, the cold, wet cloud seemed to wrap me in an icy blanket. I started an Indian war dance to warm up. "Christmas!" I finally said to myself, "No use in this. Might as well go on. I'll be sure to find Dad a little farther

*This is probably the point at which the bloodhounds lost Donn's trail, the second day of the search for him.

down!'' But I didn't find him, and the going grew rougher and rougher.

CHAPTER II

Plumes of Pamola · *First Day*

I HADN'T gone far before I *felt sure* I was down on
the plateau. I was off the trail and the going was
bad, but there weren't so many big, broken rocks to
climb over. Once in a while I came to an open space,
with moss on the ground, and I could run a little
and warm myself. I kept this up for a while and
then I ran plump into a tangle of pucker bush. Pucker
bush grows so thick that a person can actually walk
on it.* Some places I *did* walk on it. Of course, you
kept breaking through, first one foot and then the
other. That wasn't so good, but it was easier to do
that than to struggle over those big rocks. Pucker
bush is funny stuff. It hasn't any actual thorns, but
when the ends of the limbs die, they dry up hard and
brown. Boy, are they sharp!

I knew now, of course, that I was off the trail,

---

*Pucker bush is another name for wax myrtle. Its abundance and thick-
ness of growth make it almost impassable for the hiker. All trails avoid
it, wherever possible.*

and I was really anxious. I don't know how long I kept on over that kind of ground, but suddenly the pucker bush gave way under me and I felt myself falling into a deep hole. I grabbed at the bushes as I went down and got hold of a big stem.

For a moment I thought I was a goner! Boy, that hole was deep—twenty or thirty feet—and there were jagged rocks on the bottom! I just hung on to that pucker bush hoping that it would not tear out by the roots. I prayed a little, too—just hung on and prayed. I had a feeling that that bush wasn't going to break away, and it didn't.

When I pulled myself up a little and found that the roots did not tear loose, I felt around and got a toe-hold on the rock and slowly worked my way upwards. It was some job, but I did it. At last I squirmed out onto the rock on my stomach. It felt good to be safe again. I was out of breath and more frightened than ever.

I just lay there for a moment, wondering what I should do next. When I got my wind, I stood up, and I guess I must have lost my head for a while. I remember running back the way I had come, shouting like mad. I cried a little, too.

I didn't seem to mind anything. I tore through the pucker bush and jumped over rocks, falling and getting up and bumping into things. Nothing seemed to matter if I could only get out of there. When I was all out of breath, I sat down on a rock and, after crying a while, I calmed down and began to think. No use running around like that when the cloud was so thick you couldn't see where you were going. The thing I had to do was to figure out a plan and stick to it.

I remembered some of the things I learned in Scouting. First thing, I must keep my head, then, maybe, if I looked close, I could find a trail. I got down on my hands and knees and scouted around. Not a thing—not a turned-over tuft of grass—not a broken weed nor a bent twig—not a displaced stone.

"That's funny," I said out loud, "Somebody *must* have come along here, *sometime*. Maybe, if I wait until the cloud parts again, I can get my bearings". But the cloud rolled in denser than ever, and more sleet fell. I was getting awfully cold and wet.

I listened. There was a queer whining noise in the air. Sometimes it sounded like heavy surf. I tried to figure out where it came from. It might have been wind blowing in rocky caves, or wind in treetops on the timberline below. That sound made me feel creepy. I thought of Pamola, the evil Indian spirit of the mountain, and the stories the guides told about him. He lived on the mountain top—right where I was standing, perhaps. Some guides call the clouds that stream across the top of the mountain, the Plumes of Pamola. He hated his own race and, once, according to the strange tale of a half-breed, he shook his white feathery plumes over a party of redskins, and they just disappeared. There they were, one minute, shining in the sun, and the next, they were gone and nothing was left of them but clouds that dissolved into air and disappeared.

Strange that people should believe such yarns, but that's the kind of story the guides tell around their mountain campfires. Good stories, too—corkers—but I caught the guides winking at each other as they spun them for our benefit. And now, there I was, right on the spot, maybe, where those Indians had vanished. What if *I* should vanish, too? What would Mommy do and where would Dad look for me? Funny what thoughts pop into a fellow's head when he is alone with the clouds and the mountain!

CHAPTER III

SHARP ROCKS AND SLEET · *First Day*

I KNEW I couldn't sit where I was very long. Christmas! The wind was sharp, and it blew so hard that the rain and sleet stung like needles. I was getting wet all over. My fleece-lined reefer kept my chest dry, but my blue dungarees were cold and stiff as boards. Dungarees are all right for dry hikes, but they're terrible when they get cold and wet.

People want to know why I didn't stay where I was. Someone was sure to find me, they say. Well, I'd like to see anyone stay up there in that wind and sleet with the night coming on. You'd freeze stiff before morning.* I was already getting stiff. I had to keep moving, just to warm up. I shouted once more, as loud as I could—then I stood and listened—nothing but that strange noise.

*There was a terrific hail and sleet storm on top of the mountain that night, through which it is doubtful if an unprotected person could have lived. Above the timber line, a 40-mile wind was blowing and the temperature dropped to below 40 degrees before morning.

I turned slowly about so as to be sure of my direction, and started back the way I thought I had come. Pretty soon I ran right into a trail marker. It said "Saddle Trail". Now I *was* in a fix. I had heard about that trail. I had heard that it went far off into the woods and was dangerous, full of land-slides and loose rocks. However, it *was* a trail and it was marked, often with blue daubs of paint. It would lead me somewhere—perhaps to some lonely spot miles and miles from camp. No, I mustn't take it.* The thing to do is to work off at right angles to it and cut across the main trail. I started on. Right away, I ran into more pucker bush. I climbed over it and fell through and crawled under it. Guides have said no one *could* crawl under it, but I did—for a long way.

Pretty soon, I was back among big rocks again. Right here, I had a funny experience. The cloud opened for just an instant and far, far below me I saw a lake—I thought was Moosehead—shining in the sun. The cloud closed and the lake was gone and everything was dull gray again. The sight cheered me some, and I hurried faster than ever.

I started to run and found I couldn't, because of the boulders; that made me frantic and I climbed over them like a cat and yelled and shouted and cried all

Although the Saddle Trail is extremely dangerous, had Donn been able to follow it, it would have led him down to Chimney Pond (see map) where Roy Dudley's camp is located and which was inhabited that very night.

the time. I yelled for my Dad. I climbed up as high as I could on a big rock and screamed for him—then I waited. No answering shout—nothing—just the noise of that wind and the purring sound of fine sleet driving against my clothes.

I just *had* to get out of there and back to the trail. I started to run again, as fast as I could. I don't know how long I kept *that* up, but a long time—over rocks and sharp edges and things I stumbled over and into patches of pucker bush—sometimes falling and then getting up again, and often crawling under brush on my hands and knees. Boy, it was awful! And then, just when the cloud lifted again and I thought sunlight might break through, I ran into another trail sign. It said "Saddle Trail" and looked like the sign I had seen before. I was pretty scared by this time and I wasn't sure about that sign so I examined it closely. There was a mark on it that I recalled seeing before. *I had come back to the same sign.*

For a second I was stunned. I just stood there and looked at it. I knew now, for sure, that I was lost. I was running in a circle. I didn't know what to do, so I stumbled along hunting for other marks, on that same trail. I guess I went a long way over rocks and over pucker bush and sometimes under it, too, searching and hunting for another trail marker. I didn't find any, but I kept going *down*. I remember that. After a while, I came to a place where there was a lot of gravel, and boy, was it slippery! That place was dangerous, for a slip might mean a bad

fall—maybe a hundred feet or more. I slowed down. I could imagine myself lying there, in the cold and dark, with a sprained ankle. Meanwhile, the rocks were getting bigger and bigger.

At last I came to a weather-beaten tree. The branches were all pulled out to one side, as though the tree were trying to get away from something. That tree looked scared. Beyond was another and another. I had reached the timberline, and I had to find a trail, because the shrubs grew as thick as doormats and, without a trail, the going down to camp would be pretty bad.

The sight of that tree calmed me down a bit, for I began to think more clearly. It's an awful thing to get lost in the clouds. You see things that aren't there at all. Rocks look like people and shaggy animals, and often you come to an edge and think you are looking down into space, and you draw back and get scared.

The mountain suddenly seemed awfully big under me. I listened. Only the whining noise of the wind in the stunted trees—no, there was another noise—rocks falling, far off to the right—a slow, heavy, crunching sound—then silence, deeper than before.

The rocks in this place had very sharp edges and some of them were loose, too, and slid from under me. I had heard of landslides and had seen the remains of a few on the way up. I kept thinking of how a landslide starts—the slipping stones—just a few at first—then more and more and faster and faster, until the whole mountain seems to move. Then, trees tip over like matches, and there are crashings and grindings and dust. Boy! I just stood still, now and then, and shivered. What chance would a fellow have in a mess like that?

However, it was not quite so cold down there in the scrub, and that made me think that farther down, it would be still warmer. Maybe I'd better change my course a little to the right and keep going down. I hunted for an opening through the scrub growth. There wasn't any; so I just had to scramble along as best I could. That's where I cut my sneakers to pieces.* I noticed now that I had to scramble through more and more of those scrubby bushes. My face was badly scratched and I was awfully tired. It was getting dark, too.

I knew I hadn't covered more than three or four miles. That meant that Dad and Henry couldn't be a long way off. The camp must be right down below me in the trees. I felt a little better. What if it *were* hard going down to it? A fellow *could* make it, as long as he didn't break a leg or something. I'd just go a little more slowly—that's the way a fellow

---

*"The stones are so sharp on parts of Mt. Katahdin," says veteran guide Earl W. York, Jr., "that a pair of new, heavy sneakers will not last over six trips, even when the regular trail is followed."

figures things out. I was all wrong, of course. There wasn't any camp below *me*—not for miles and miles, and there weren't any trails where I was going.

It's a good thing I didn't know any more than I did. Sometimes, not knowing the worst helps a fellow along, if he just keeps going and doesn't lose his head.

The trees grew taller and taller. Going was easier than at first, and the air was warmer and not quite so soaked with mist. There was no sleet. I could see a little ways ahead—just broken mountain side with bushes and trees everywhere. No use to shout now. No one could hear me. Just one thing to do—work my way down to the camp. Maybe I'd be late for bacon and beans, but what of it? Dad might be mad because I didn't stay with Henry and the man, but he wouldn't hold anything like that against me very long.

Just as I was thinking over such things I slipped off a big rock and hurt myself. I lay at the base of it, kind of stunned. At last, I got on my feet again. I saw that night was falling. The woods were clearing of mist but getting dark. I knew it was raining, but where I was, the trees protected me a little, though drops kept falling and wetting my hair. I thought over what I ought to do, for a long time, then I decided to sleep right there for the night.

Before I bedded down under a big tree, I scouted

around a bit and found a small stream. I knew then I was near the foot of the mountain. I was hungry. Boy, I wished I hadn't eaten all my raisins on the way up. A raisin would have tasted good. I was thirsty, too, so I took a drink. Then I took off my sneakers and dabbled my feet in the water. Christmas! I was surprised. Those sneakers were slashed all over.

When my feet felt better, I got up and started towards the tree. On the way back I saw a cave. It looked deep and dry, but I was afraid of it. I picked up a rock and threw it in. I could hear it bounce, inside. Nothing happened. I thought it would be a good place to sleep in—to get out of the cold and rain, but I was afraid of some animal coming home in the night; so I passed it up and went back to that big tree. It had two roots that ran out like arms. I got a little moss together in the hollow and lay down. I curled myself up into a ball and pulled my reefer down over my legs. The dungarees bothered me. They were wet and cold and as stiff as boards; so I got up and took them off. I put them and my sneakers under an old rotted tree trunk to keep them as dry as possible.

I said my prayers and lay down again and shut my eyes. I was more comfortable but awfully wet and cold and hungry.

Things look different at night in the woods, especially when a fellow is alone. Maybe a First

Class Scout, who had timber experience, wouldn't mind, but I did. I listened for a long time. Some queer bird screamed in the distance. Something fell on the mountain. A frog croaked. The mosquitoes were thick, too, and I kept slapping them off my face and neck. At last, I stripped off my blue shirt and wound it around my head. My fleece-lined reefer covered me down to my waist, and I could draw up my legs under it, too. My feet gave me the most trouble. I couldn't cover them very well and they were awfully cold.

I kept thinking of Mommy and Dad and wondering about them, and then I said some more prayers and felt better inside. I felt that God would help me if I needed help. I woke up once or twice and, each time, I wondered about Mommy and Dad. I felt awfully sorry about what had happened, for I knew Dad was out on the mountain somewhere looking for me.* I knew that up on the top it was cold—pretty near freezing—and I blamed myself for not sticking close to Dad and the boys on the hike up. If I had done that, I would be safe on my cot-bed in camp. I cried myself to sleep.

When I opened my eyes again, it was morning, and rain was still falling—but not heavily. I couldn't figure out for a moment where I was, then I re-

---

*As a matter of fact, Mr. Fendler and a small searching party were already looking for the boy, at this time. For a complete description of the organized hunt in which several hundred persons took part, see "Afterword."

membered. Just below me was a little open space through which the stream ran. Beyond it was an old stump, all hazy with mist and the drizzling rain. I was shivering and unhappy.

CHAPTER IV

Ghosts on the Mountain · *Second Day*

HENRY CONDON is a strong boy. He is seventeen, I think, and he likes to help a fellow. When we were climbing up to the top of the mountain, I got tired and he took me on his back and toted me for a long way. I remembered *that*, before I went to sleep, and Christmas! I wished I'd never left Henry up in those clouds. Henry would have found his way down, because he's the son of a guide and knows everything about the woods. He knows what berries to eat and what kind of mushrooms are good and what kind are poisonous. I guess I must have dreamed about Henry that first night, because when I opened my eyes and saw that old stump down by the stream, there he *was*, too. I could see his head, but his neck and shoulders were hidden by the stump. Boy, was I glad!

You may think this was a dream, but it wasn't. My eyes were wide open and I saw everything. I *know* it wasn't a dream, even though it sounds crazy now. I sat up straight and yelled, "Henry! Henry! Here I am! Come and get me!"

Why didn't Henry answer me? I wondered about that. He was so still there behind that stump and he had such a queer look in his eyes. He was scared, and that made *me* frightened, too, because Henry wasn't afraid of anything. He wasn't afraid of noises in the woods and he just laughed at bears and things. I tried to get up to go to him and I did get onto my knees, but something had happened to my legs. They weren't legs at all. They were boards and my knees had iron hinges in them. So I just stayed there, leaning on my hands, and looking at Henry. Watching Henry was enough to scare the daylights out of a fellow. His eyes seemed to be popping out of his head. They never winked. They just stared down stream.

I had to do something. "Henry," I screamed. "Here I am! Don't you see me? Come and get me! I can't walk. I can't get up!"

Then, when Henry didn't even look at me, I turned half around and saw why. Christmas! No wonder Henry was scared. Over there near the stream, in a clear place, were four white figures—they were men, and big men, too. Each had on a long white robe that went right down to the ground and they all had white hoods over their heads, with the peaks pulled out in front so I couldn't see their eyes. They had eyes, though—I know that, because something seemed to blaze under the hoods, like the eyes of cats at night when a headlight picks them up on the road.

Each one of the men had a long arm stuck out towards Henry. The arms were partly covered by white sleeves, but they were partly bare, too, and skinny. I knew then what was happening. Those men weren't going to let Henry help me. They were hypnotizing him, just like a fellow I read about once in a book.*

"Henry," I screamed, "Don't *let* them! Look at *me!* I'm here, near a tree." I began to cry, because Henry wouldn't answer me. Just then, a man on a black horse rode out of the thicket on the other side of the brook. He was smiling and I thought he was going to rescue Henry, but he rode right along and disappeared. Right after him came a black automobile. I knew then what had happened. Boy, was I happy! Dad had come for me. I was so glad that I cried, and I held onto the tree and pulled myself up onto my feet and shouted, and Dad answered me. "Donn, Donn!" he shouted.

*No amount of questioning could shake Donn on this point. He repeatedly used the word "hypnotize" to explain the action between Henry and the men, steadfastly maintaining that he was awake, that his eyes were wide open. Probably, never again in the course of his wanderings did the boy approach so closely the brink of insanity. Fear, loneliness, hunger and the fall from the rock—the results of which were undoubtedly more severe than the boy realized—all contributed to this temporarily unstable state of mind.

"Here I am, Dad!" I yelled back. I got my legs going and started towards the brook. I went right by Henry and I must have frightened the four men, because they disappeared like smoke.

I was pretty wise, too, because I remember fishing my dungarees and sneakers from under the old tree and taking them with me when I ran towards Dad. I waded into the water and, boy, was it cold! It made me shiver all over. I stumbled on a slippery rock and went down on my hands, and the water splashed into my face. It felt good, because my face was hot with so many blackfly bites. I got onto my feet and scrambled up the bank. Nobody was there. Henry was gone. Only the old stump stayed where it was. The automobile was gone, and though I yelled till I was hoarse, nobody answered me. Dad was gone, too. I just sat down on the ground and cried.

I don't know how long I sat there and cried, making my hands go up and down on my knees, but pretty soon I felt weak all over and so I stretched out on the bank and put my head on my arms. I got to thinking about Henry and the four men and I thought about them for a long time. "That's the way people go crazy," I said to myself. "That's when they start to run and tear off their clothes." Well, I wasn't going to go crazy—not if I could help it.

One thing kept going through my mind all the

time I lay there on the bank. I learned it in Scouting and it did me a lot of good—maybe saved my life. "Keep your head and you'll come out all right— just keep your head!" When I had made up my mind on that point I felt better. There wasn't any Henry to help me, and there wasn't any automobile, and Dad hadn't called me. I was lost and that was all there was to it. It was better for me to get going and get myself out of the mess I had blundered into.

It's queer what funny things go through a fellow's head in a fix like that. There were times when it seemed to me I wasn't talking to myself at all. Instead, somebody inside of me was doing all the talking—somebody who wanted me to get out of those woods and go home to Mommy and Dad. Somebody who would keep me from going crazy if I just listened.

After that little rest on the bank I felt better. It wasn't quite raining, but it was dark and misty and I felt cold and miserable. I remembered that I hadn't said my morning prayers, so I got onto my knees and prayed. I never prayed like that before. Other mornings I hurry a little or don't think much about what I am saying, but *this* morning I meant everything, and I thought of God and how He was there in the woods, and how He looked after everything, and I felt warm all inside of me and peaceful, too.

When my prayers were over, I thought of putting

on my dungarees, but they hurt my legs; so I threw them over my arm and picked up my sneakers. Christmas! Those sneakers weren't much good to me. When I tried them on, they were so tight and hurt my feet so much, I had to take them off. I guess the rain had shrunk* them way down. So I tied the strings together and hung them over my arm with the dungarees. Then I went down into the brook. It was just a little brook, but it flowed pretty swiftly. As I waded into it, I recalled a Scout rule. "When lost, follow a stream down. It will lead to a larger stream, and there are always camps along the larger streams." That's the way I remembered the rule and the talk the Scoutmaster gave with it. That advice sounded good to me and I decided never to leave the bank of the stream, even if I had to scramble over rocks to keep to it.

Maybe you think it wasn't hard work following that mountain stream. Boy! The going was slow and painful! My feet weren't tough like Henry's and the water soaked them and made them even softer, and the rocks I had to walk over weren't like pebbles at all. They were flakes of stone, like Indian arrowheads. I had to teeter along over them like a boy walking on a tight rope. Sometimes, when the water got too deep for wading, I had to hug the bank and crawl on hands and knees under the brush.

*The rain and dampness may have shrunk Donn's sneakers—but it is more than probable that those sneakers, shrunk or not, would no longer fit the boy's swollen feet.

Maybe that's how I lost my sneakers. Anyhow, I came up from one of those crawls and my sneakers were gone. I wondered what I should do, but when I sat down and looked at my feet, I knew sneakers were no good to me. I couldn't put them on even if I had them. My right foot had a cut on the side and was bleeding and the nails on my left foot were all broken, and one was bleeding badly. I had hurt my left ankle, too, scraping it against a rock, but that didn't bother me a great deal.

Well, the sneakers were gone. I shrugged my shoulders*—no use to look for them, just a waste of time. Anyway, shoes didn't seem important. I don't know why, but they didn't. I knew I'd find a camp just around the bend. I could stick it out till then,— anyone could. I'd just go a little slower, that's all, and be a little more careful, a fellow had to, for those rocks were sharp. I whistled a tune. I had to laugh a little at myself as I whistled. I'd heard Dad speak of people whistling to keep up their courage and I guess that's just what I was doing.

*A very characteristic remark that throws a flood of light on Donn's acceptance of circumstances and conditions. He has a habit—when puzzled—of shrugging his shoulders, pursing his lips and lifting his hands.

CHAPTER V

BLACKFLIES ARE NO FUN · *Second Day*

MOSQUITOES have always bothered me. Even one in my bedroom will keep me awake, but on that mountain. Boy! And those blackflies! Swarms of them—like clouds. Christmas! Somebody ought to do something about those blackflies. They're terrible—around your forehead under your hair, in your eyebrows and in the corners of your eyes and in the corners of your mouth, and they get up your nose like dust and make you sneeze, and you keep digging them out of your ears. I don't know how long I walked fighting them off and trying at the same time to pick soft spots for my feet, when I suddenly felt weak all over. I was hungry. I knew I would have to find something to eat. I left the stream and went up into an open space that looked like an old pasture. I saw berries there on bushes that looked to me like blueberries. I was about to eat some of them when I remembered that Dad had told me, "Never eat berries unless you're sure of them, especially the blue ones." I wasn't sure of these blueberries. I never had picked any; so I passed them up and went back to the stream and drank a little water instead.

About the middle of the afternoon, I sat down on a big rock to rest. Boy! I was a sight. My wrists were covered with blood from the mosquitoes I'd smashed, and my feet and legs were all red, too, from the cuts and scratches and bites. I had a million bites. I looked like I had measles or smallpox. I got a little worried when I found my feet were numb. I pinched my big toe and didn't feel anything.

I wished I had a hat with mosquito netting around it, like some of the fishermen in the camp wore. I wished that, because the blackflies and mosquitoes didn't give me any rest. They made me so nervous that I could have jumped out of my boots, but I didn't have any boots to jump out of. I could hear their wings and they sounded like airplanes right in my ears. I felt like getting up and running, but what good would *that* do? They'd follow, and I'd pick up others. Anyway, they were only flies and not bears or wild cats. They couldn't kill a fellow, even if they could drive him nearly crazy. I pulled my dungarees up over my legs and lay back on the rock, and I guess I slept for an hour or so because the shadows were pretty dark under the trees when I awoke with a start.

Something had happened. I couldn't tell just what. There had been a loud noise, like a snort and then a scramble as though some creature had gone away fast. I didn't dare get up. I just opened my eyes and looked about as far as I could without moving my head. All was quiet, except the growling of low thunder in the mountains somewhere. I was glad of one thing—the drizzling rain had stopped. I lay there listening for a long time, then I sat up and looked around. Down near the stream edge, in the mud, there were hoofmarks, quite large ones, and they were fresh because water was oozing into them. Then I knew what had happened. A deer, maybe a moose, had come up close to me while I slept.

After my rest on the rock, I felt much better. I bathed my feet in the stream and, while doing so, did I see some trout! If the fishermen in the camp knew about those trout, they'd wear their shoes out getting to them—great, green fellows with pink portholes, sliding through the water like eels—just a flip of a tail and they went a yard. Those trout looked good to me. I hadn't eaten anything since the morning before and I was hungry. I lay over the rock on my stomach and watched them. Maybe I could catch one with my hands. Nothing doing! They slid beyond reach each time, but they weren't frightened at all. They just hung around watching me. I guess that shows that they hadn't been fished much.

Anyway, what could I do with a raw trout? I couldn't cook it because I didn't have any matches. My Dad is strict about that. He never permits us boys to fool around with matches at home or in the woods. Even if I had matches, a whole box of them, and they were all dry, I would have been pretty slow about lighting a big fire where I was. A hurricane must have gone through that region, for there was down timber everywhere—whole patches of "blow-downs," as the guides call them, with the tops all heaped together like the makings of a bonfire.* I knew very well what would happen if those tops got going—the whole place would be a roaring furnace. A fellow wouldn't have any chance at all. So I didn't worry much when I couldn't catch a trout because I don't like fish anyway, and I couldn't eat it raw.

Night was coming and I was pretty tired. I wasn't so much afraid now, but I wondered why I hadn't run into somebody or come across some trail. Tomorrow it would be different, and I'd be back with Dad. Maybe I could just telephone to Dad to pick me up on the way to Caribou, and we wouldn't lose much time after all.† That started me to thinking about home and Ryan. I missed Ryan a lot. He's my twin and he'd know what to do, because he's level-headed and smart.

Maybe he was out playing with the other boys, right at that moment. While I was thinking over such things, I found a gold mine—no, not exactly a gold mine, but a strawberry patch—big berries, too,

*A windstorm wraught considerable havoc on Mt. Katahdin in 1932. Donn refers to the results of this storm.

†Mr. Fendler had promised the boys a trip to Caribou, following the ascent of Mt. Katahdin.

and as sweet as honey. Did they taste good! I got down on all fours, like a bear, and gobbled them as fast as I could. I guess I ate a few leaves, too, but that didn't matter. Pretty soon, I noticed darkness setting in. It gets dark fast in those woods.

I have always been used to going to bed early. My Mommy and Dad think that children need lots of sleep. Maybe that was a good thing for me, because when bedtime arrived, I always stopped and hunted for some place to sleep.

Just before I found the berrypatch, I came across an old stump with a lot of green moss around its roots. That seemed like a good place to sleep so I went back to it. My dungarees chafed me so badly and were so wet and cold, I took them off and shoved them under a small log that was leaning on a rock.

Maybe you think a fellow can't curl up in a ball when he's cold! Well, I had my knees right up under my chin. I got my knees under my reefer that way, and that helped keep the mosquitoes off. Boy, was I dumb! I never thought of piling moss over my legs or pulling down some branches. Maybe I could have made a lean-to if I had known how, but I didn't, and anyway, I was awfully tired and my hands were sore from catching hold of rocks and rough branches all day.

It's easy to think up things to do, *now*, but it was different in the woods. Maybe you think I didn't miss a good bed. That moss wasn't soft at all. There was always a stone under it sticking into my ribs. I'd lie on one side as long as I could, and then I'd turn over and that would give the mosquitoes a new start. Those mosquitoes were terrible. Maybe turning over so often was the wrong thing to do, but I did it.

I went to sleep right away that night, but I didn't sleep long. It began to rain—great big drops that woke me up. I listened for a moment, shivering all the time and crying a little from the cold. I could hear thunder, but it sounded way off and kind of hollow. Then it started to rain harder and harder, and I remembered a hollow tree I passed. I stumbled back towards it. Boy! Was it dark! I could feel the fleece in my reefer getting wet, and I didn't like that. I was in such a hurry that I forgot my dungarees. At last I found the tree and crawled in. It was bigger than I thought and I was able to curl up in a sitting position. It was dry and warm in there, and I just thanked God for being so good to me.

Then, I dropped off to sleep.

CHAPTER VI

I HEAR FOOTSTEPS · *Third Day*

I DREAMED some wild dreams that night, but I can't think of *one* of them. I wish I could. Some of them were funny, and some scared me. I can remember that much.

When morning came, I tried to crawl out of the tree. Now I know how an old, old man feels, going around with a cane. I couldn't move. I had rheumatism, and my knees creaked like old hinges. My neck was stiff and sore, and I had a pain down the middle of my shoulders. I wondered if pneumonia began that way, but I took a long breath and didn't feel any pain so I knew my lungs were all right.

Outside the sun was shining. I lay still and watched it for a long time. A little brown bird came right up to the tree and started to hunt for bugs among the roots. I could see the sunlight on its feathers and I remember saying to myself, "This can't be such a bad place after all. That little bird seems to like it." When the bird had flown away I worked my way out of the tree. Boy, that was some job!

The sight of that bird eating grubs made me hungry and so, after going over and looking at my dungarees I left the stream and went back up on a little hill where some bushes grew. I didn't put on the dungarees, for when I felt of them they chilled me, they were so cold and wet and stiff. I just shoved them back under the old tree trunk.

On the hill I found some berries. They were pretty dry, but I ate all I could find, then I remembered that I hadn't said my morning prayers. I didn't want to start the day that way, so I knelt down and prayed for quite a while. You see, at that time I didn't really think I was in a bad fix. I knew I was lost, but I expected to run across someone fishing or camping around every bend in the stream. That's the way it is, you keep saying to yourself, "Well, I'll find somebody around the next bend." You keep saying that to yourself all day long. It never came into my head that a fellow could get so badly lost in the United States of America, and that days would pass without seeing a soul.

After I had said my prayers I went down to the stream, found my dungarees and threw them over my arm. I waded into the water, hugging the bank as much as I could. I did that because the ground there was not quite so hard on my feet. Every little while I would come across a sandy place where I could straighten up and walk fast.

As I went along, I came to a big rock—a piece of granite, I guess, that had rolled down from the mountain. On the shore side of it was a patch of bushes so thick that I could not force my way through. On the stream side the water was so fast and deep that I knew I could not wade it. I had to crawl to the top of that boulder and then jump a big crack to another rock.

I forgot to say that by now the brook had become quite a stream. I don't know how many little brooks had run into it, but I know I crossed over quite a few.

I got to the top of the boulder, all right, but I hurt my wrist doing it. I sat down on top to rest and that gave me a chance to watch the water rushing between the rock I was on and the one just beyond. That water gurgled and gurgled and churned and seemed to be trying to climb right up to me. I was pretty stiff, but I knew I had to jump; so I tossed my dungarees across ahead of me. In one of the pockets, I had a big piece of rock.* I was carrying it back to Mommy from the top of Katahdin. Maybe she'd use it as a paperweight or a doorstop. That rock was

*This rock was heavy, very heavy, and yet Donn had carried it under almost impossible conditions for a day and a half. He had picked it up for his mother as a souvenir from the top of Mt. Katahdin and it never occurred to him—even though it might make the going easier—to throw it away.

heavy, and I knew Mommy would like it; so I carried it along.

Well, I didn't have strength enough to toss my pants clear across onto the rock. The legs hit the top all right, but the pocket with the stone in it slapped onto the side with a dull thud. And there my dungarees hung for a second, slowly slipping, inch by inch, into the white water, racing below. All I could do was watch them slip. Why didn't I jump across and save them? I don't know, except that I must have had a feeling that the least touch or jar would shoot them into the stream. Maybe, I was just paralyzed, looking at them. Boy, what a moment! What would I do, if they slipped into the water? How would I keep off the insects? How would I ever get into camp without being seen? Well, I figured that I could crawl into camp after dark, when everyone was in bed—maybe.

While I was thinking such things, down slid the dungarees like a fat, blue snake into the water. One leg flapped up against the rock and they were gone. I couldn't believe it. My pants were *gone*. There I was like a kewpie or something. It might be all right to run around in the woods like that, but what would I say when I came around a bend and found a camp? I couldn't walk in like that and say, "I'm Donn Fendler. Please telephone my Dad I'm here." Everybody would die laughing.

Well, maybe after that, anyone would expect

me to hunt for my pants. I didn't even look for them. I just jumped across to the other rock and went on. Maybe I could have found my pants—I don't know—but by the time that day was done, I was glad I had lost them. I couldn't slap blackflies and mosquitoes and mooseflies with heavy, wet dungarees over one arm.

I kept pretty close to the stream the rest of that day. When the shadows darkened under the trees I began looking for a place to sleep. I was lucky. On a little bank, about a hundred feet away from the water, I found a beautiful patch of soft green moss under a pine tree. I was tired but I took the time to pull a lot more of the moss together and spread it out into a bed. I said my prayers and lay down. I couldn't go to sleep right off, so I watched a bird with long legs fishing near the edge of the water. He would run a little and then stop and cock his head on one side and look and then run a little more. Then he would shoot his long bill into the water and spear a tiny fish. Boy, I wished I could feed myself as easily as that!

Suddenly I heard footsteps right behind me. I didn't move. Something snorted, then a deer stepped past me so close that I could have touched it and went down to the brook. I must have made a noise of some kind, for the deer suddenly stopped and turned its head and looked at me, then it wheeled around and faced me. I never saw such big eyes. I stayed as still as a mouse. I wasn't frightened, either. I wanted to see what that deer would do. Pretty soon it took a step towards me, then another and another. I wondered if it would walk on me, but it didn't. It looked and looked, then snorted and banged up and down with its front feet. Then it turned and went down to the stream and took a drink.

I can throw a baseball pretty straight, and there were plenty of round stones handy, but I didn't want to kill that deer. I felt glad it had come, and I felt glad that it wasn't afraid of me. I watched the deer for a long time. When he had gone, I closed my eyes. Just before I went off to sleep, I thought of a glass of milk—a big, cold glass with white foamy milk in it. Boy, the juice just ran down the corners of my mouth thinking of it! Anybody who doesn't like milk is crazy.

The brook was pretty noisy right there, and it sounded like someone humming a tune. I went to sleep listening to it.

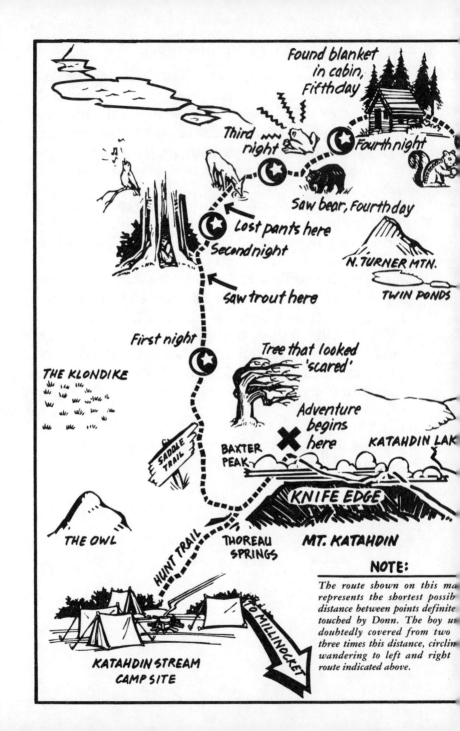

CHAPTER VII

BEARS ARE NOT SO BAD · *Fourth Day*

I HAD plenty of dreams that night—maybe you never chased your pants all over the lot and never could catch up with them because they could run faster than you could. Well, that's the kind of dream I had, and I must have been thinking a lot about my pants, because when I woke up, the backs of my legs were as sore as though I had slid down a rock and taken the skin off. The skin was off, too, but I had done it myself in the night, scratching mosquito bites. Christmas, was I sore! The red, deep scratches burned like fire and a million blackflies and mosquitoes bit right into them.

It's bad enough in the woods to have a whole skin for bugs to peck at, but get a break in it and see what happens! That's when you run into *real* trouble. I guess flies are just lazy, and a cut saves them the bother of boring in. Anyway, I woke up with every cut and scratch lined with insects. Even the ants were having a picnic on me, but the worst pest of all was the moosefly. You wouldn't think a fly *could* bite like that fellow. He lands and zingo—you're bit and the blood is flowing.

The flies were so bad in that place that I knew I had to get out of there in a hurry. It was sort of swampy, with water standing between rocks, and when I got down on my stomach to drink from the stream, I noticed black, slick bloodsuckers all over the bottom. I wondered why the trout didn't feed on those bloodsuckers. There were millions of them.

As soon as I had washed myself, I started away from the stream to escape the flies. I went towards an open space I could see above me through the bushes. The stream had cut into the bank at that spot, and I had some trouble climbing up the steep side, but I made it. When I crawled out on top, on all fours, *was* I surprised! Four or five deer were feeding right out in the open! They looked up and saw me, but didn't seem the least bit frightened. They just moved over to one side of the open space and watched me. Now and then, a buck would snort and make his front legs prance up and down.

I looked around and found strawberries there, and I ate some. Then I saw some bushes that were full of blue and green berries. I didn't eat any, but I got down on all fours and picked the strawberries that grew in between the clumps. Those strawberries were good. I thought of cream, and that made me think of milk, and that made me think of Mommy and Dad, and I cried while I was eating the berries.

I was pretty lonesome, too, and getting discouraged. Besides, I wasn't as strong as I had been the day before. I had to work harder to get through the brush and once, when my jacket was caught in a thorny vine, I had trouble getting it loose.* I almost gave up. That vine was so strong, it tore pieces out of my jacket and scratched my legs till they bled. Anyway, I got out of that fix and began to eat strawberries again. I had worked down close to the stream once more, and I noticed that it made quite a noise over the rocks.

Suddenly, as I came around a clump of berry bushes, I came face to face with a bear—a big one, black as ink, and standing on his hind legs. I was stooping over, and when I straightened up, the bear saw me and screamed like a person. Christmas! That scream just turned me cold. I couldn't run. I couldn't yell. I couldn't do anything. I just stood and stared, crouched over a little, because I never finished straightening up. For a second, that bear and I just looked at each other, then the bear made a big leap sideways. I don't think he touched his forepaws to the ground. He just went sideways as though on springs and splash!—whish!—bobbing up and down, with the water flying around him, he was on the other side of the stream. *Was* I glad! I straightened up and laughed. I couldn't help it. I just laughed and laughed, and then I cried and tears

*Undoubtedly horsebrier, a tough, wiry vine growing in dense clumps and covered with the sharpest and strongest of thorns. The thorns hook inward, slightly, and are particularly dreaded by all unprotected woodsmen.

ran down into my mouth and then I laughed again. That bear stood a while looking at me and then he got down on all fours and loped off with his black shoulders going up and down like a horse on a merry-go-round.

I couldn't eat any more berries—I wasn't hungry any more. I just wanted to get into the next camp and find someone who would telephone to Dad. I was getting worried about that trip to Caribou. I didn't want Dad and the boys to be cheated out of it because of me.

My feet were bothering me a lot, now, and I was lame. Something in my hip hurt me when I walked. Besides, every time I stepped on a stone or a broken twig, I'd have to cry with pain. I guess I cried a lot that morning. I tried not to, because I knew I had to keep my head, but I did, and I guess that wasn't so bad, because guides have told me they cried, too, when they got lost in the winter and had to "hole up" for a day or so in a snowbank.

When I was feeling worst, I got down on my knees and prayed. I had to hunt some moss, because my knees were so sore they almost made me scream when I went down on them, but I found the moss under a tree and I prayed as hard as I could. I prayed out loud, too, asking God to help me, because I needed help and asking Him not to let Mommy and Dad worry and asking Him for food—just something to keep me going till I found a camp and, oh, yes, I asked Him to help me get out and not let my feet go back on me. I had to ask Him about my feet because my toes were so stiff I couldn't bend them. They stuck straight out and the ends were cut and worn, and my left foot had a slice cut right out of it.

After I had prayed, I rested a while. Then I got up and, right around a big rock, I found a road. It was just a tote road into a camp, but it was a road just the same and easy to walk on. Here and there, logs had been laid across, corduroy style, and water stood between them, and it was cool there, with beautiful green ferns growing. I knew the road was an old one because there were no signs of any horse or wagon wheel.

I was happy at last. I knew that road would lead me either into a camp or out to another road. I didn't care which; so I followed it, going as fast as I could.

CHAPTER VIII

I Find a Cabin · *Fifth Day*

THE FLIES and mosquitoes were pretty bad in that place because the ground was low and swampy. At first I beat them off, but pretty soon my arms got tired and hurt me so to swing them that I just went on, letting the flies bite. I remember, once, when I slapped down on my wrist, the blood splashed into my face.*

I don't know how long I followed that road, but night came and I had to stop. I picked out a place under a tree and tried to go to sleep, but the

---

*Men experienced in the Maine woods testify that this is no exaggeration. In addition to the mosquitoes, blackflies and moose flies that made Donn's life miserable, there are two other common varieties that unquestionably did their part to make him uncomfortable—copperhead flies and another variety, almost invisible, called by the Indians "no-seeums." Of these insect pests, veteran guide Harry Kearney says, "The moose flies are by far the worst, but the bite of a copperhead—a tan, translucent fly, about half an inch long—can cause blood-poisoning, unless cared for immediately."

frogs kept me awake. Boy! They must have been big ones. One would croak and another would answer him. They were arguing—and arguing always makes me feel like running away.

"You did," one frog would say. "I didn't," would answer the other. "You did," "I didn't," "You did," "I didn't"—until I had to get up and go away from there. A handful of stones would have come in handy, but I didn't have any stones and anyway it was so dark in there you couldn't see your hand before your face. I had to go mighty slow, feeling the road with my feet, to keep from bumping into something.

After a while, I came to an opening. I could see the stars. Right in the middle, on what seemed to be a mound, was a big tree. I crawled up close to it and dropped down, too tired to go another step. I slept hard, too, for it was broad daylight when I awoke. Something was talking to me. I couldn't make it out for a long time, then I opened my eyes and a chipmunk was standing on a limb with his tail jerking up and down, looking at me. He was saying a lot, too, asking me what I was doing there and if I were lost and telling me to cheer up, that a camp was just around the corner and there was bacon frying and maybe an egg or two.

Funny how you can get chummy with the wild animals when you're in the woods. I had to laugh at that chipmunk—he was so busy talking, with that tail of his jerking up and down all the time. I found out that the woods creatures don't want to hurt you, and they'd all help you if they could.

I just lay there and listened—and laughed a little. It didn't seem to me that I could ever get up. I tried to lift my head, but it just plopped back like a head made of putty. I closed my eyes and dozed again, and then I rolled over and pulled myself up by hanging onto the tree. It sounds funny, but I wasn't glad another day had come.* I was sorry, because I had to walk some more and my feet were so sore and covered with cuts and bites that every step made me yell out. That was at first, but a person can get used to anything, I guess. After my feet got warmed up, it wasn't so bad.

I would stop, now and then, when I found a patch of wet, green moss, and just stand in it. Boy, it felt good!

The little chipmunk seemed to want company, too, for he followed me like a dog, only he went along in the trees over my head. He kept chattering

*At this point in his story, Donn was asked, "But weren't you glad to see daylight come?" His answer was a definite and emphatic "No!" Day, to him, meant only torture on the road, throbbing feet, burning bites, hunger, anxiety and the fear that every step was taking him farther and farther from civilization.

all the time. He was a pretty little fellow, and I wondered why he went so far with me.*

I hadn't gone far along that tote road, maybe two or three miles, when I knew I was coming to a cabin. First, I saw a pile of tin cans, sort of a dump, but the cans were all rusted, and you couldn't tell what kind of cans they were.

I stood and looked at them. Even a rusty tin can looks good to a fellow lost in the woods. It shows that someone else has been there, ahead of him. Not far from the pile of tin cans I saw some rusty iron barrel hoops hanging over a limb, and then the road turned and I came right out onto a clearing.

Christmas! That was a glad moment for me. I was kind of stooped over, I was so tired, and I thought sure someone would come running out of a door and say, "Hello, where did *you* come from!" But nobody did.

I stopped a while and looked things over. The cabin was made of logs and the bark had partly

---

A study of Donn's wanderings (see map) brings only astonishment at the amount of mileage covered by the boy each day. The distance from Baxter Peak, down the North Peaks Trail to Wassataquoik Stream and, following it, to Lunksoos Camp, is approximately forty-eight miles. But the guides who heard Donn's story and re-created the route he must have followed estimate that the boy covered at least twice this distance—perhaps, three times—making from ten to fourteen miles a day over difficult wilderness terrain.

peeled off, but the door was closed with a latch—
at least that's how I remember it. There wasn't
any bacon smell, like you generally find around
camps. Then I knew what had happened. The camp
was deserted and I wasn't much better off than before
I found it. Still, there was a house there and a fellow
might find something to eat on a shelf, something
someone had forgotten—a can of beans, maybe, or
evaporated milk. Boy, wouldn't *that* be good—a can
of beans!

I hurried as fast as I could. I lifted the latch
and the door almost fell off its hinges. That scared
me and I pushed it open, slowly, and peeked in. I
didn't know what was in there—a porcupine, maybe,
or a skunk. There wasn't anything like that, but how
that door did squeak! The inside of the house had a
funny, musty smell. There was a bunk along one
side, but it was empty. There was a bed, too, with a
mattress on it and a rough blanket covering the
bottom. That bed looked good to me but I was so
hungry that I went straight to the cupboard.

There were cans on the shelves. One was a
brown match box, but it was empty. I opened
another can—coffee. I opened another can—salt.
I opened another can—empty. They were all empty
after that, but I found two pieces of iron, a part of
a big knife and a bar of some kind. They were up
on the top shelf. I cracked them together and boy,
what a spark! I did that three or four times and,
every time, I got a spark. I thought of stories I had

read about people lighting fires with sparks and I thought I would try it.

I had a good reason, too, for wanting a fire. I forgot to say that when I came near the camp I looked into the brook—I guess I took a drink—and it was full of the biggest trout I ever saw—big, blue fellows, all headed up stream. Boy, were they lazy! They just floated in the water and looked at me. I guess they knew I didn't have a hook and line. If I'd had a hook and line, they would have gone off a mile a minute.

I thought of those trout when I made those sparks. I hit the pieces of iron together again and made *lots* of sparks. It was almost like having a sparkler. I thought that was fine so I went outside and got some dry cedar bark and crushed it all up in my hands. I worked it back and forth into a loose ball. Behind the cabin was a place where there was no wind. I put the ball of cedar bark on the ground and crouched over it. Then I struck the two pieces of iron together as close to the bark as I could. But I didn't get a spark. I got sparks inside, but I didn't get any outside. I thought that was funny. I went over to the cabin and got some dry, fluffy stuff from between the logs. I tried the iron pieces, again—no sparks—nothing.*

*When it was explained to Donn that, in the semi-darkness of the cabin the sparks would be vividly visible but, in the bright sunlight outside, would not be noticeable, his comment was, "Boy, wasn't I dumb!"

I FIND A CABIN

Well, I couldn't start a fire. I worked hard at it, until my arms got so tired lifting the iron bar that I could scarcely move it. I gave up trying and it didn't seem to matter at all. I thought of the trout and then I thought of the trouble it would be to catch one. Maybe they only *looked* lazy. Maybe if I started a big fire the wind would get it away from me and set the whole forest going. I thought of that and of the signs I saw on Katahdin. That mountain was plastered with yellow signs asking people to help prevent forest fires. Dad had pointed them out to me and we had talked about the timber damage every year from fire.

I went back into the house and took the blanket off the bed. Christmas! I got a fright when I pulled it off. Boy! There was a mouse on it with long ears.

He squealed and hung on so tightly that I had to take him by the tail and yank him off. I thought mice were afraid of people, but this one wasn't. He was just mad and he wanted that blanket as much as I did. Then I wondered if I was stealing it. I thought of that mouse and the owner of the blanket. I wanted to take the blanket with me, but I wondered if that would be the right thing to do. I thought of Dad. What would *he* do? Would he be mad if I took it along? I remembered what he always told me, "Never touch a thing that doesn't belong to you." Dad wasn't thinking, maybe, of me, lost in the woods. Still, something seemed to tell me to go ahead—that the owner would *want* me to have it and the mouse could find something else to sleep under next winter.

While I was folding it, I came across a big safety pin—the biggest safety pin I ever saw. I remember I took it in my hands and couldn't believe it was a safety pin. When I tried to snap it shut, though, I found it didn't go hard at all.

That safety pin made me think of the trout again. I could make a fishhook out of it. All I had to do was bend it into shape. I did a lot of thinking about that, but finally gave up the idea. I couldn't eat raw trout.

I folded the blanket into a bundle and took it with me. What a smell! It almost made me sick. Then I went out of the cabin and started down the road. I went about a mile and a half and, boy, I got sleepy! I was so sleepy I just staggered. I spread the blanket out in an open space on some sort of green vine with berries on it. I never smelled anything so bad as that blanket. I almost had to hold my nose, but I went to sleep just the same. The sun was shining and I lay on my stomach with my cheek on my arm and only my blue shirt covering my back.

CHAPTER IX

I Hear An Airplane · *Sixth Day*

A GENTLE breeze was blowing across that hill and it kept the flies and mosquitoes away from me. For once I was free of them. I'll never forget how warm and comfy that blanket felt. The cuts and bites on my legs seemed to stop hurting. My feet felt warm and safe and even my toes softened a little as I fell asleep. That was early morning.

When I woke up, the sun was way down on the other side. I had slept all day, and boy, did I feel good! I sat up and wondered what to do next, then I noticed something was the matter with the backs of my legs. They smarted and pained as though I had sat down on hot coals. I got up and examined them. The skin was as red as paint and all hot and fiery-looking. Lying there in the sun for so many hours had given me the worst sunburn I ever had. After that, for a long time, I found it more comfortable to keep going than to sit down to rest. I put on my reefer and threw the blanket over my arm.

It was awfully heavy but I had to have it. I remember I carried it a long way.

Just as the sun was sinking I came around a bend in the tote road and saw something that made my heart jump with joy. There, right in front of me was a telephone wire nailed to trees. I shouted and danced and laughed and then I cried some. I was saved at last. All I had to do was follow it. It would lead me straight to some camp. I looked at the wire. It didn't seem *too* old. Since it led into the tote road at that point, I decided to keep going just as I was. Boy, the sight of that wire running along ahead of me gave me a lot of courage and cheered me up a good deal.

That night I crawled under a down tree and curled up in my blanket. I didn't feel so bad. But I was hungry, my head felt hot and I had queer dreams. I dreamed I was in a New York automat with a lot of nickels in my hand.

I'd put in a nickel and down would drop the door on a ham sandwich. Then a hand would reach in over my shoulder and take the sandwich. I'd move on to a big piece of lemon meringue pie and drop in a nickel. Down would drop the door and, before I could reach in, a hand would go across my shoulder and take the pie. Pretty soon I had used up all my nickels and hadn't had a thing to eat. That was pretty tough and I wanted to get mad, but I couldn't. I just went out for some more nickels.

I woke up after that dream and stayed awake a long time. The wind was making noises in the trees—like a storm coming. I didn't like the sound of that wind. It wasn't friendly, like the cheeping of the chipmunk. Pretty soon I knew the dawn was coming. Creatures began to move in the forest. I couldn't see them, but they were all about me. I closed my eyes and wished night would stay forever. I never was glad to have the day come.

Suddenly I heard a chipmunk cheeping over my head. I opened my eyes and there he was, the same chipmunk I had seen the morning before. I knew he was the same one from the way he jerked his tail and bent down and looked at me.

As soon as the road was light enough to travel over, I got up and folded my blanket and started on. First, though, I said my prayers. I prayed hard, too, and I felt that God wanted me to get out—but He wanted me to do it on my own legs. I prayed and cried and hollered for food but nothing happened, so I figured food wasn't so important, after all. I'd find some more strawberries and they would be enough. After a while, the tote road went up on a higher level and I *did* find berries in a little open space—a few—and I spent a long time picking and eating them.

After I had eaten all I could find, I went on for a long way. There were high trees overhead most of the time. I was down on my stomach getting a drink from the stream when I heard a low hum. I listened. It sounded to me like an airplane, but Christmas, no airplane would fly over *that* timber. What *for?* The humming grew into a roar. I tried to find an open spot. Maybe, if I could *see* that plane, the pilot could see *me*. I ran and ran. I stumbled on the logs laid across the road and fell. Then I went lame and could only hop along on one foot.

Pretty soon I knew I couldn't find any place where I could see that plane, so I stopped hopping and listened. That plane just zoomed right over my head and died away across the trees. I knew then that Dad was looking for me. Things must be pretty bad when they had to get planes. I sat down beside a tree and cried.

I must be lost for sure, when even a plane couldn't find me. Maybe it was no use to go on. Maybe there wasn't any camp for miles and miles. Maybe that telephone wire didn't go any place, after all. Maybe I was following it the wrong way, to another abandoned camp. After I'd cried a while, I knelt down and prayed. I wanted the plane to come back. I wanted to hear the noise of its motors—but it didn't come back. I got up and went on, still a little lame. Now and then I could see the sky. Clouds were piling up and I felt it was going to storm.

I picked up the blanket. It was awfully heavy. It made me stagger. One end slipped down and I stepped on it and it tripped me up. I fell and hurt myself. I left the blanket where it dropped and went on. I had to find a camp that day—I *had* to find it. I *had* to find it. I knew I had to find it because my legs were stiffening up. I walked on like a man on two wooden legs, just one leg out and then the other, one leg and then the other.* Something was happening in my head—something terrible. I was falling from somewhere into a black pit, between jagged rocks, with millions and millions of blue streaks going past me like shooting stars. I was trying to call someone but couldn't make a sound—just falling and falling.

The next thing I knew I woke up and it was getting dark.

I was sitting on a rock looking at my feet. They didn't seem to belong to me at first. They were the feet of someone else. The toenails were all broken and bleeding and there were thorns in the middle of the soles. I cried a little as I tried to get out those thorns. They were in deep and broken off. I wondered why they didn't hurt more, but when I felt my toes, I knew—those toes were hard and stiff and had scarcely any feeling in them. The part next to the big toe was like leather. I tried to pinch it, but couldn't feel anything.

---

*The agony of Donn's every movement at this point is clearly understood when it is realized that his feet, by now, were a mass of cuts, each one inflamed and some infected. His knees were badly swollen and thorns in the instep of each foot were later removed at the hospital in Bangor.

My head ached and I didn't want to move, but night was falling and I had to go on, at least as far as some big tree. I got to my feet. Was *that* hard! I could scarcely bend my knees, and my head was so dizzy, I staggered. I had to go across an open space to the stream, and as I went along, I saw a big bear, just ahead of me. Christmas, he *was* big—big as a house, I thought—but I wasn't a bit scared—not a single bit. I was glad to see him.

When he got nearer, I knew he didn't see me, so I crouched down a little behind some bushes—but kept my head up so that I could watch *him*. I didn't want him to run right into me. He ate berries, as he went along. He'd swing his head and nip one way and then he'd swing his head and nip the other. He kept making grunting noises. I don't see how he ever came so close to me without seeing me, but I kept mighty still. I hardly breathed. I knew I was a goner, if he took after me. I couldn't run or climb a tree—not with those feet and legs. Pretty soon, he dropped down on his front feet and I couldn't see him any more, but I could hear him, breaking down the bushes as he went away.

CHAPTER X

Ever See A Swink? · *Seventh Day*

BOY, I WAS lonesome when he was gone. I
cried some and sat down and ate a few berries,
and then I got up. I didn't go very fast now—kind
of picking my way from soft spot to soft spot. I had
to take care of those feet—and *were they sore!* The
flies bothered me, too. I always carried my blue
shirt over my arm, so as to protect my head with it
if those bugs got too bad, and I was doing it now.
That left only my reefer on my back, with the fleece
inside.

Those flies, the black ones, crawled up into the
fleece and bit me all around my waist and around my
neck—every place an edge showed. That was bad,
for I couldn't do anything but slap myself, and pretty
soon I got so tired slapping, I just quit and let them
bite.

I found the road all right and the telephone
wire, too. It was cooler but there were more bugs—

mosquitoes as big as flies. I watched one fill up like a balloon and then drop off, too heavy to fly.

Even with my blue shirt tied by the sleeves around my head, those mosquitoes bit me on the forehead and eyelids. I had to peek out to see where I was going. Sometimes my eyelids swelled up, and I was afraid I wouldn't be able to see any more.

Pretty soon I came to a fork in the road. The telephone wires went off to the left and a trail went off to the right. The stream was on the right, and I was afraid to get away from it for fear I wouldn't have any water to drink. Every time I had left the stream, I had to go without water. I never found any springs or any other water fit to drink—just pools in rocks with green scum on top. I knew better than to drink any of that. I never drank any scum-water all the time I was in the woods.

I stood for a long time thinking what to do about that fork in the trail. I tried to think what Dad or Henry would do about it. Finally, I guessed Henry would keep to the stream, because, if a fellow did *that*, he couldn't help coming out somewhere. Besides, there had been a big storm over that country and hundreds of trees were down. What if the telephone wire ran into one of the "blow-downs?" What would I do, then?

Well, no "blow-down" could plug up a stream and stop it from flowing. I decided to leave the wires and keep to the water. I was getting pretty weak by now, so when I reached the stream I got down on my stomach and took a drink. There were bloodsuckers in that water, but I didn't care. I drank a little and rested my head on the moss.

That chipmunk was still following me and he came and chattered on a limb above me. But I didn't pay any attention to him. I was too tired. I rested up a bit there and went on. I remember looking at my arms when I tried to get up. Boy, they were skinny! My arms were always strong, even if they weren't big, but now they were just bony and so weak I could hardly make them work. I knew I had to get some food soon, but I wasn't hungry any more.

I missed the easy going on the tote road. The brush was very thick and so I had to wade in the water most of the time. I waded and scrambled and crawled until I couldn't move another leg, then I lay flat on my stomach and rested.

Once, as I went along, a stone turned over under my feet and I fell and hurt my hip. I thought, for a moment, it was broken, but the rush of the cold water around me made me struggle to get up and I found I could move my leg. Just below that spot I came to some rapid water. I was limping and, trying to get closer to the bank, I stumbled and fell head foremost into the stream. I rolled over and over. My fleece-lined reefer filled up and my head went under the water and I had a feeling I was going to drown. Over and over I rolled, striking against rocks and scraping over the rough bottom.

Just below me was a long sandbar on which grass and a few bushes were growing. I got my feet under me as I went past it and reached out for the bushes. I didn't get hold of them but I *did* pitch forward and fall down in shallow water. I was so scared and tired, that it took me a long time to crawl up the sloping bank and stretch myself out on top of it.

The sun was shining and it was warm, there. I don't remember much after that, for a long time. I must have gone to sleep, for when I woke, the sun had gone way down.* I hated to move, but knew I had to. No one could sleep out on that bar. To my surprise, my reefer was almost dry.

I took it off and spread it out on the hot sand. Then I searched along the edges of the stream for an open space, in the hope of finding a few berries. There weren't any, so I picked up my reefer and went down stream. I made pretty slow time. I was lame and afraid of falling into the water again. It seemed

*This entire episode is reconstructed from the boy's fragmentary memories of this particular experience. Without question, Donn kept going, overcoming difficulties on the way, in a semi-automatic manner during the final forty-eight hours before he was found. He was emaciated, starved, frightened, tired to the point of complete exhaustion—but his mind, after the second day, remained normal, except as fatigue clouded it. This is clearly indicated by the bright shafts of memory that continually pierce that cloud.

to me I wasn't getting anywhere at all. That evening, I went to sleep early—on some moss under a tree.

It got cold that night, and I couldn't double up as tightly as I did other nights because my knees were too stiff. That left my feet out and, by morning, they didn't have any feeling in them at all—not one bit. I woke up once in the dark, shivering. I curled up tighter and tried to sleep, but I couldn't, for a long time. I kept thinking of Mommy and Dad and that airplane. I thought I heard another plane, but, of course, I didn't. People don't fly over that place at night. It was just something in my head—maybe, a mosquito near my ear.

There were funny sounds, though, in those woods—things walking, something big and heavy—and something drinking—and the funniest noise I ever heard, a high, quavering screech that made your blood cold.* I guess it was a bird, for pretty soon the noise came from another spot. There were other noises, too—like trees and branches breaking and crashing down.

After a while, I fell asleep again, and I dreamed of a swink. Maybe you don't know what a swink is,

*Probably a screech owl—maker of one of the most eerie sounds to be heard in the woods at night. It is remarkable that Donn does not, in his narrative, make greater reference to night sounds. The probable explanation is that he was so exhausted each night and slept so profoundly that he heard little. If this explanation is correct, he was protected from a hundred terrors. Wilderness woods are filled with night noises that are terrifying to the inexperienced.

but it looks like a pig—has big ears like a camel and has a long snout like an anteater. It is death to bugs and eats them up so fast that pretty soon there aren't any. I read about it once in a book of comics. Boy, I had a swink, and it was a beauty and what a job it did on those bugs! First it licked my legs clean, and then it licked my arms and it even licked my face and neck. I never had anything feel so good as the tongue of that swink.

It took me a long time to wake up. I'd keep waking up and falling asleep again. When I did finally get my eyes wide open, I couldn't make up my mind to go on. I was afraid that day would be just like all the rest.

CHAPTER XI

WHEN I DID get on my feet I found they were only stilts. I felt I was standing way up in the air. I didn't dare walk much for a while, because I was afraid my feet would just fall apart and leave me walking on my bones. That's the feeling I had.

I rubbed my feet and then put them in the cold water of the brook and, after a while, a little color came into them and I could feel a pinch. When I could walk, I left the stream and went out into the sun and it felt good. I looked about for some strawberries, but there weren't any. So, after I warmed up a little, I went back to the stream and started down with only a drink of water for breakfast.

Boy, if I'd known what was just around the bend in that stream, I wouldn't have waded into that water. I climbed up on a rock to avoid a deep trout hole and I guess I was too weak to make it, for I found myself sliding off into the water. I tried to hold on to the rock, but it was pretty slick, and off I went, clear up to my neck. That wasn't so bad, but the water was icy cold and I was still shivery after the night. For a second, I was too surprised to move. Then I floundered around and climbed out on a sandbar on the other side of the stream.

I felt something wriggling on my legs and looked down. Christmas! I was covered with little, black bloodsuckers. I knew them, for I had seen them before. They were all over me and they made me so scared that I began to yell and scream and jump up and down. I have always hated things like that and can't bear to have one touch me. I guess I went wild for a moment. I scratched and tore at them. I couldn't brush them off and I knew, if I didn't, they'd swell up worse than mosquitoes. I don't know why I jumped back into the water, but I did, and I thrashed around and rubbed myself with sand, and when I came out, nearly all the bloodsuckers were gone.*

Maybe some Scout Leader can tell me why they went away in the water. There were a few left and I picked them off as fast as I could. There was a spot

---

*There is reason to believe that, before Donn crawled out of the stream and on to this bar, he fainted and lay partly submerged in the leech-infested water. This would give the leeches opportunity to fasten themselves to his body. In his weakened condition, the sight of them may have caused the boy to faint again, on the sand bar. Exposed to the sunlight and completely out of the water, the bloodsuckers—as he calls them—would then, undoubtedly, drop off.

of sun on that sandbar. I was so tired after my battle with the bloodsuckers that I lay down full length and closed my eyes. I dozed off, I guess, for I had queer dreams, none of which I can exactly remember. These dreams weren't like seeing Henry, the first day. These were *dreams*—but I *saw* Henry, all right, with my eyes wide open, that first day.

When I awoke, I felt better. I picked my way over the stones and got up on the bank. Right away, I found what looked like a trail. I followed it, going very slowly. I think I was just a little crazy, for I kept looking around to see if anything was after me, and here and there I'd start to run.

After running a little, I'd get out of breath and then I'd stop and lean against a tree until I felt better. I was having trouble with my legs. They would shake and quiver, all the time, but especially when I stood still. Boy, it's a queer feeling to have your knees quivering under you as though the bones had been taken out of them!

Now and then, terrible, dark feelings rushed up into my head, like the one I had before I fell asleep. I can't describe these feelings, but they were always dark and empty, but with something in them you couldn't locate—something that made your heart pound and your legs want to run.

I don't know whether I ought to tell something that happened that very morning, but I guess I shall. It's all right, of course, but people who don't believe as I do, may think it's all imagination. I believe in Guardian Angels and, on my trip through the woods, one of the things that comforted me and helped me to bring myself out to safety was this feeling that I wasn't entirely alone.*

In the night, in those dark woods, that feeling helped me and, in the daytime, when the going was awfully hard, I felt as though I had someone to lean on, and that helped, too.

Well, after I struck that trail and had gone along for a quite a way, I tripped over a root and fell down. I was flat on my face. I couldn't get my arms under me,—they were so weak at the elbows. I just lay there and waited. Suddenly, I felt something take hold of me by the shoulders—something like strong, gentle hands—and I felt myself lifted slowly until I was on my knees. I looked around, expecting to see a man, a guide maybe, and was I surprised when I could see nothing—not a thing! But the hands were still there and they were lifting and lifting. I got first one foot under me and then the other, then I straightened up. I was stronger. I could walk.

Well, I hadn't gone a half-mile before I saw something hanging from a tree. I went over to it and found a gunnysack nailed to the trunk. It was old and rotten and had a hole in it, but it made me think of a sleeping bag. I took it down and threw it

*In discussing this with Donn, later, his father said, "Your Guardian Angel must have been helping you." Donn replied, "He was pulling me along."

over my arm with my blue shirt. Boy, that bag came in handy right away! The mosquitoes flew up from the stream in clouds, and the blackflies were just about as thick. I put the gunnysack over my head and peeped out through a hole. That helped keep off the bugs, but it made me stumble and, boy, every stumble hurt! It seemed as if my head would burst, every time I pitched forward.

I pretty nearly passed right by some old cabins, because of that sack. It wouldn't have mattered anyway, because when I turned off the trail into the clearing, I knew there was nobody there. The cabin doors were falling off their hinges and weeds were growing on the doorsteps. The roofs were caved in and green with moss.

I pushed in one of the doors. The place smelled musty and damp. I went inside and put down my things and thought I'd take a rest. I stretched out on a bunk and closed my eyes. I thought, because of the roof and walls, the bugs wouldn't bother me. That's where I was wrong. They came in armies, big ones and little ones, and they lit all over me so thick I seemed to be covered with pepper. Boy! That was the worst place I was ever in. I got up as fast as I could and grabbed my things and went out.

A wind was blowing across the clearing and that scattered the bugs a little. I felt pretty bad. I wasn't getting any place, after all my walking. It seemed that everything I came to was deserted. I began to wonder if I'd make it and began to wonder, too, if people were looking for me, why I hadn't heard a shout or the sound of a gun or seen some sign. I knew the Boy Scouts wouldn't let me die in there without hunting for me and I wondered why I hadn't seen any of them. Boy, what funny things come into a person's head! I thought if I saw a Boy Scout, I'd ask him for a doughnut and a drink of milk. I thought so hard of doughnuts that sometimes I could smell them.

I wandered around those camps for a while looking for something to eat. I looked in all the old cans I could find. They were all empty. No use hanging around there. I got my things together and went on. After that, I lost track of what happened. I can't remember much—things are hazy, like dreams you can't describe afterwards.

It was that afternoon, I think, that I discovered part of my big toe was gone. I can remember that. I was stumbling along the trail. Now and then I was down on my hands and knees. It was easier, that way, when my feet got so bad that I couldn't bear my weight on them. Suddenly I looked down and saw that the tip of my big toe was gone—cut right off and the blood was coming out fast. I don't know how it happened. I never felt a thing. I must have hit a sharp rock or walked over a piece of glass in that camp. I sat down on a stump and held my toe in my hand. I held it tight, to stop the flow of blood. I held it for a long time, then I got up and went on.

SOLDIERS IN A SWAMP

I remember finding a hollow tree and sitting with my back in it and my blue shirt over my legs and the sack around my head. I got warm there and, maybe, that is where I spent the night. You may laugh at that "maybe," but all I can remember, after that, is finding myself walking close to the stream on a level place where the grass was soft.

I couldn't tell whether it was another day or not, for I got all mixed up about where the sun ought to be. I remember looking at the water close to me, to see which way it was flowing. It wasn't wild and rushing any more. It was spreading out, getting wider, and there were reeds and cattails. I could see the sky, then, and it was full of big clouds. I listened and watched for an airplane, but all I saw were big birds, like wild geese, going overhead.

Pretty soon I stepped into some water and went up to my knees. That scared me and made me back up. I climbed onto a tree trunk and I could see a big bog full of dead trees. Each one looked like a soldier. The sun was shining on them and some of the branches looked like silver. I had a queer feeling about those trees—they didn't want me to go that way—they were on guard there, blocking my path. They didn't want me to go on.*

*This entire swamp episode is confused and uncertain. Donn, at one time, denied that he got into a swamp at all. At a later time, he was certain that he did. It has seemed wise, however, to include this second version of the episode, realizing that the boy, reaching the limit of his remarkable stamina, was probably—to use a pugilistic term—"out on his feet" for hours at a time.

CHAPTER XII

Journey's End · *Ninth Day*

THE FIRST thing I really remember after that, I was standing looking down at a big rotten tree. I still had my blue shirt and gunnysack, but I seemed like somebody else. I was just watching myself do something. I saw myself crawl under the leaning trunk of the rotten tree and curl up into a ball. My legs went into the gunnysack and the blue shirt went around my head.* I was on a merry-go-round, going 'round and 'round and up and down, and I tried to hang on for fear I'd fall off, and then, I guess, I fainted because I never knew anything more until the next day.

I can't remember much that happened when I woke up. I couldn't see very well for a long time. Maybe that was because the sun was shining in my

---

Donn has a strong feeling that this gunnysack actually saved his life. It was, of course, invaluable in keeping the insects away from his bare feet and legs—especially, at night. He still has the sack and treasures it, with good reason.

eyes. When I tried to get up, I couldn't make it. I was sick to my stomach and my head ached. I knew I had to get up, though, for the flies were getting bad and my cut toe hurt me a great deal.

When I couldn't get up, I started to say my prayers. I prayed for a long, long time, and I remember what I said. It was just the same prayer I had made before. I asked God for four things. I asked him not to let Mommy and Dad worry too much, and then I asked Him to take care of the other children, and then I asked for food. I asked Him out loud for food because I hadn't had any for such a long time. I knew it was Sunday, and that made me "lost" a whole week.* I wanted to go to church but, since I couldn't, I decided to say longer prayers. I think I prayed for an hour.

The fourth thing I prayed for was someone to come in and get me. I prayed as hard for this as I did for food, because I knew I was getting weaker and weaker.

After I had prayed, I looked around for food, maybe an acorn or a red berry that I could reach. Nothing happened. There wasn't anything I could eat. I expected to find something and I was so disap-

---

*It is clear, here, that the boy had completely lost track of time. Instead of being lost for a week, at this point, he had wandered for the greater part of nine days. When asked why he had not kept track of the days by tying knots in a piece of long grass, or by notching a stick with a stone, he replied that he expected to find his way out any moment, the first two days, and that that feeling continued with him, from day to day, after that.

pointed I started to cry. When I had cried a long time, I stopped and just lay there looking up at the sky through the branches of the trees. Something inside of me kept urging me to get up, and I'd try, but could never make it.

I guess I fell asleep for a little while. When I awoke I felt better and I worked until I got up on my feet. Christmas! I could hardly pull one foot after the other. That was at first; later, little by little, I found I could walk easier, and pretty soon I could go right along. The worst of it was when I fell down—then I'd lie just as I dropped for a long time. I remember I felt dazed and kept turning my head this way and that. Then I'd get up on my knees and, pretty soon, I'd get onto my feet again. Every time I fell I'd say, "Maybe I can't get up this time," but I'd pray a little, and then I'd get up. Praying always helped me to get up.

That's the way things went for a long time. Then, after I'd pulled myself through some bushes, I saw white water ahead—I mean, open water. I just stood and looked at it. I couldn't believe it, because I knew if I found a pond or lake, I'd be all right. So I just stared, and pretty soon I made out a shore line, not very far away. Close to the bank, floated a big log. I had to look at one thing at a time, because it was hard for me to see at all. Things were hazy and wouldn't stay still, but that log gave me new courage and steadied me a lot. It looked like part of a wharf.

I had to go around a dense clump of bushes to get to it—and there, across the water,* was a log cabin.

When I looked across and saw that cabin I couldn't believe it. I stood right where I was for a long time. I was afraid it was like all the other cabins I had come to. Still, it looked new and there was an open space in front of it. While I was standing there, things kept going through my mind. What if it were deserted like the rest? Well, I'd just go on. Then I wondered how I'd ever get to it. It seems funny to me now, but I felt sure I could swim across. I'd tie my blue shirt and reefer and gunnysack on my head, somehow, and dogpaddle over. That didn't seem a hard thing to do at all—but where would I get a piece of string?

I crawled under the bushes and came out on the bank. I could see the cabin better now, and there was a big elm tree right near the edge of the clearing and boy, oh, boy, two canoes were turned over on the ground. Canoes! There must be people there— fishermen, likely—and they'd help a fellow any way they could. They'd give me something to eat, maybe some bacon and beans, or a doughnut, and then I could find the way back to camp and maybe get there before dark.

While I was thinking things like that—and I

*Donn had reached the East Branch of the Penobscot River. See map.

guess I was blubbering some, too, because of my feet—I saw a man come out into the clearing!

I crawled out on the big log so the man could see me, and began to yell. I guess that yelling was pretty funny, for Mr. McMoarn told me later it sounded to him like a screech owl.

I yelled and yelled and waved my arms. I saw the man look over towards me, then run into the house. "Christmas!" I said to myself. "What's the matter with him?"

While I was wondering, I saw him come out of the house again on the dead run, with other people after him. I saw them slide one of the canoes into the water. A man yelled to me to stay where I was, that they were coming after me. Then I knew I was saved, and I got kind of weak all inside. I had to get off that log. I had to get off quickly, because I felt like falling over in another one of those sick spells I had back in the woods. Maybe I *did* faint, too. I don't know, but the next thing I remember a big man was picking me up. He didn't say much— just shook his head and picked me up.

He was going to leave my gunnysack, but I grabbed it just in time. I wasn't going to lose that. It had saved my life. I guess Mr. McMoarn asked me some questions, but that's all hazy in my mind. The next thing I really remember was Mrs. McMoarn. She was grand. She took me in her arms, and she

was crying and saying things, and she laid me down on a bed and began telling people what to do. I heard the telephone ringing like mad, and then Mrs. McMoarn came over to me with a bowl of soup. I don't know what kind of soup it was, but it was good.*

I wanted to drink it right away, but they wouldn't let me. Boy, try eating warm soup out of a spoon when you haven't eaten much for nine days! Mrs. McMoarn was slow giving it to me, too, and I just couldn't wait for the next spoonful. I tried to get hold of the spoon myself, but she said that would never do and that she was feeding me exactly the way the doctor ordered over the phone.

I guess I fell asleep, while I was eating that soup, for the next I knew, noises of people waked me up. Boy, the room next to me seemed filled with people, all whispering together and moving around. Someone was talking very loud on the phone. Pretty soon, Mrs. McMoarn came in and smiled at me. She said they were trying to get my Mommy on the phone. Then Mr. McMoarn came in and said everything was

*The soup must have tasted good—for this twelve-year-old boy, four feet, seven inches tall, weighed approximately 74 pounds the day he was lost, came out of the woods weighing 58 pounds. He had lost 16 pounds in nine days. To this note should be added the report of Dr. Ernest T. Young of Millinocket, who examined the boy a few hours after Donn reached the McMoarn camp: "His body was covered with scratches and insect bites, which apparently were giving him no little discomfort, and he was unable to rest upon his left hip because of an abrasion. In spite of his hazardous experience, his general physical condition seemed exceptionally good."

ready, and he took me up in his arms and carried me out into another room where the phone was. I heard a voice, but, honest, I didn't recognize Mommy at first. Her voice didn't sound natural at all. Maybe it was the crazy wires nailed to trees.

But when I really listened, I knew it was Mommy.

She was crying and talking, too, and asking me if I were really safe, and I told her, "Sure, I am all right. I just had a bowl of soup." Then I asked her about Dad, and she said he was right there. Boy, it was good to talk to Dad. I don't know what I said, but I was glad just to know that he was there listening to me and that he wouldn't have to worry any more.

I guess Mr. McMoarn thought I had talked enough, for he took me away from the phone—but I hung onto it as long as I could.

When I was back in bed, and they had all gone out for a little while to let me rest, I remembered God. I hadn't thanked Him for all He had done for me. So I just closed my eyes and said my prayers and thanked God for kind people and for His help back there in the wilderness and for a good Mommy and a good Dad.

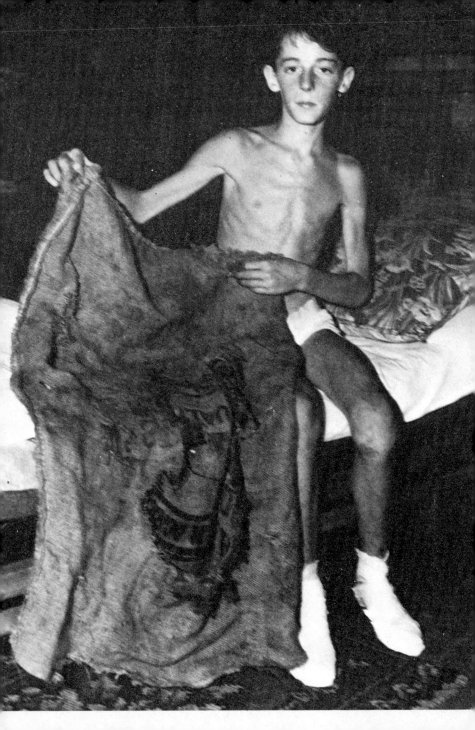

Afterword

THE STORY of Donn Fendler's experience would not be complete without some description of what took place in the outside world during the nine days he was lost. That story begins with the significant moment when Donn decided to leave Henry Condon on Baxter Peak and go back down the Hunt Trail, alone, to rejoin his father.

The man near the Knife Edge, to whom Donn refers, was the Rev. Charles Austin. He joined Henry Condon on Baxter Peak, within ten minutes of the time Donn had left that spot to go back down the mountain. Because of the dangerous cloud condition, the two immediately started down the trail. As Donn had had a ten-minute head start, they were not surprised that they did not catch sight of him and, it was not until they had joined Mr. Fendler, about a mile down the mountain at the edge of the plateau, near Thoreau Spring, that they realized Donn was lost.

Mr. Fendler and Donn's younger brother, Tom, had just left the spring and were starting ahead on the last mile to Baxter Peak. They were waiting there for the return of Donn and Henry Condon and, in the thin mist that surrounded this whole part of the mountain, they mistook Mr. Austin and Henry Condon for Henry Condon and Donn. In fact, Tom remarked to his father, "Doesn't Henry look big in the fog."

Of course, as soon as they were within clear vision, Mr. Fendler shouted, "Where is Donn?" After a moment's consultation, all agreed that Donn had missed the trail. The party immediately started back on the plateau towards Baxter Peak—Mr. Fendler and Tom keeping close together and Mr. Austin and Henry Condon separating, so as to cover every bit of terrain possible.

As they hurried back, they called continually for Donn, not believing that he could possibly have wandered off the plateau in so short a time. After about an hour's frantic search, during which time the sun had gone down and semi-darkness descended, it became evident that Donn had strayed quite a distance from the plateau itself and that more searchers were needed. A quick consultation was held, and Mr. Austin insisted that *he* stay on the plateau, while the rest of the party go down the mountain to the camp, at the base, for assistance.

Henry, who was thoroughly familiar with the

mountain, immediately ran on in advance of Mr. Fendler and Tom, and was soon out of sight. Tom and Mr. Fendler were well worn out and, being unfamiliar not only with Mt. Katahdin but also with mountain climbing in general, had to go down at a much slower rate.

Henry reached the camp at the bottom of the trail and explained to the Forest Rangers what had taken place on the mountain. A small party was organized, and the following account, published in the Revere, Mass., *Journal*, July 27, 1939, gives a vivid idea of what took place during the next few hours.

"Monday morning, July 17, the party I was with started to climb to Mt. Katahdin's lofty summit. I had climbed many of the peaks of New Hampshire, including Mt. Washington, both day and night, so I regarded this ascent as just another climb. Before I had reached the summit, I was fully convinced that Mt. Katahdin's ruggedness had been grossly understated and that I was climbing the toughest mountain east of the Rockies. I arrived back at the base camp in mid-afternoon and promptly fell asleep.

"About 7:30 that evening I strolled over to the Rangers' tent to inquire about the other trails that ascend the mountain, their location, length, and so forth. We had talked scarcely ten minutes when a young boy, in the most exhausted condition I have ever seen, came running down the trail.

"It was some minutes before he could speak to tell us that a twelve-year-old boy was lost on the tableland, a 40-acre plateau, high on the mountainside!

"Within fifteen minutes, the Ranger and I, along with four others, were winding our way up the six-mile-long trail. A short way up, we met the lost boy's father, who supplied us with more detailed information. He said that he, with his two sons and another small boy, had started to climb to the summit of the mile-high peak. The youngsters raced ahead, and Donn, the missing youth, had turned to go back to his father but had lost the trail.

"With cheery assurances that we would return with the boy in a few hours, the searching party continued on up. Darkness fell upon us shortly before we reached the tree-line where we found two fellows camping for the night. Here we paused for a brief rest.

"Far below in the blackness a light burned, the only sign of human habitation in the vast wilderness, and also the signal that the boy had not been found. Two lights would have called us back. One light spurred us on. Above us, shrouded in heavy wet clouds, lay the tableland and still above that, rose the peak.

"We started again. From here on, the climbing became increasingly difficult. Irons driven into stone provided us with hand and footholds to assist us over otherwise unscalable boulders. The clouds enveloped us in a penetrating dampness, the wind increased, a light rain fell, and the rocks became slippery, thus slowing our pace. The sides became steeper and seemed to fall away on each side into mist-filled bottomless pits. I shuddered to think of the little lad's possible fate.

"We reached the Gateway, the beginning of the tableland, before 10 o'clock. To reach this point in daylight, the average climbing time is two and one half hours. We had made it, in pitch darkness, in less than two hours!

"Here we split into parties of two and spread out, fan-like, over the broad tableland. We flashed our lights in the scrub, under huge boulders, over rocky crags, and between great splits in the rock, calling out for the little fellow constantly, and straining against the wind to hear the feeble cry that never came.

"In all my life, I have never been in a more desolate place. The wind was blowing 40 miles an hour or more. The temperature hovered around 40 degrees, although I could swear it was less. My hands had grown numb from the cold and I swapped my flashlight from one hand to the other. Rain and sweat ran down my face. My shoes, stockings, and pants were covered with mud from searching through rain-drenched grass and brush.

"My feet began to ache. My legs ached. My back, my knees—I ached all over. My heart set up a terrific pounding in my ears. I was wretched. I thought of the Indians and their God of Evil, Pamola. Surely, Pamola reigned on his lofty throne that night.

"With lights that stabbed the fog and darkness a mere twenty feet, we worked our way along the rim of the tableland to the edge of the Saddle Trail. How the Ranger, Dick Holmes, knew the way in that sea of blackness, I shall never know. We went down over the edge. The trail was made up of small stones, sharp and jagged, and offered insecure footing. We slid and fell too many times to relate.

"It was after midnight when we finally reached another Rangers' cabin on the other side of the mountain. To our disappointment, there was only one occupant of the place, who promptly arose and gave us hot coffee and food. The young fellow sleeping there quickly dressed and he and the Ranger started back up the mountain within fifteen minutes— each carrying packs of supplies for those still searching on top. Before leaving, they instructed me to listen carefully, as long as I could keep awake, and also cautioned me how to handle the boy should he be out of his mind and put up a struggle when I approached him. I maintained my vigil until drowsiness overtook me.

"I awoke early next morning, and gazed upon a mountain spectacle I had never seen before, for all my activities had been on the other side of the summit and at night. Cliffs of ugly rock rose up straight 350 feet, and here and there large patches of snow clung. I shuddered again and thanked the Lord that the Ranger had known the way and led me along the edge of that chasm and safely down the only trail on this side.

"My right foot pained terribly as I hobbled for five miles through the wilderness, keeping my eyes glued to the telephone wires to make sure I kept to the right trail. Where the trail met the road, I was welcomed by a friend who drove me back to our camp, twenty miles around the mountain.

"It wasn't until two days later, when a Millinocket doctor snapped them back into place, that I knew that the joints in the arch of my foot had come apart during that hazardous search on Mt. Katahdin."

Early the next morning, Mr. Fendler, who had spent most of the night searching frantically with the small group on top of the mountain, got in touch with every agency possible to get a large group of searchers under way. The Forest Service and all its branches throughout the Katahdin district were notified. The Great Northern Paper Company, which operates large timber crews throughout this section of Maine, sent about twenty "cruisers" from their Greenville station, and men were sent in from Island Falls, as well. These "cruisers" are expert woodsmen who know this section of Maine from long experience. Chief of Police Allen Picard, of neighboring Millinocket, and Mrs. Bernice Buck, of the Board of Selectmen of the same town, spread the news rapidly. Within a few hours, there were hundreds of people on the mountain. Men even left their jobs at the paper mill in Millinocket to join the hunt for the missing boy.

The Maine State Police had two bloodhounds which were immediately rushed to the plateau and which picked up the scent of the lost boy. The bloodhounds led the searchers to Saddle Spring, where the trail was lost. It was the general consensus among the searchers that Donn had left the plateau and had fallen down somewhere between the big boulders which surround the plateau on all sides. The two bloodhounds were not accustomed to the rough terrain and their feet were soon torn and cut to such an extent that they had to be taken back.

Many people thought that the bloodhounds would have found Donn if their feet had not been so cruelly torn by the jagged boulders over which they ran. A phone call was made to New York State asking for more dogs. Two were rushed by plane and arrived at Katahdin on Wednesday morning. As a precaution, leather shoes were strapped on their feet to save them from the torture suffered by the other dogs.

Inasmuch as the National Guard could not be

called out without the Governor's explicit command, communications were established with Governor Barrow's office. He was in California, at this time, and it was not until about four o'clock Wednesday morning that he was finally reached. The order was rushed through, and sixty-five National Guardsmen joined the search.

With such a large force on the mountain, provision had to be made for feeding the searchers. A National Guard field kitchen was sent up from Bangor, and the Great Northern Paper Company sent one of its field kitchens, called a "wangan", to Chimney Pond, located at the base of Baxter Peak on the other side of the mountain.

The hunt was divided into two groups—one in charge of Earl W. York on the Greenville-Millinocket tote road side, and the other one in charge of Roy Dudley, veteran Maine guide, on the Chimney Pond side. The State Forestry plane was pressed into service and, for two days, flew over the mountain and surrounding country. This proved to be merely a gesture, however, because from the height that the plane had to travel, the boy could not have been seen.

During the first five days of the search, from Tuesday to Saturday, no attempt was made by the searchers to look below the timber line. It was felt by all the veteran woodsmen and guides that Donn could not possibly have gotten down off the bare mountain that first treacherous night. In fact, it

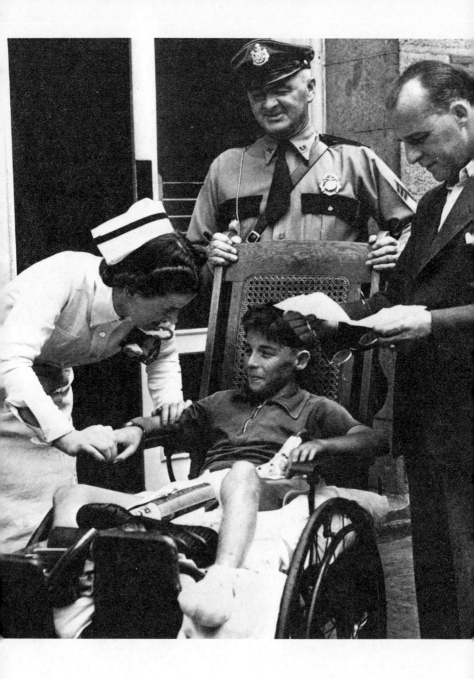

was generally believed that the boy had perished.
The hunters, then, were searching only for his body.
The crevices between some of the boulders were
thirty to fifty feet deep, and the searchers, traveling
about twelve feet apart, looked into every possible
hole where the boy could have fallen. It was not
until late Saturday that Mr. Fendler, who had a strong
feeling that Donn had reached the timber line and
was still alive, was able to convince the searchers
that possibly he was lost in the wooded section
somewhere below the timber line.

Sunday, the army of searchers, numbering between four and five hundred individuals, began to
give up the search, and only faint hope was held out
for the boy's rescue. Mr. Fendler never gave up
hope, however, even though no encouraging clues
had been found since the bloodhounds lost Donn's
trail on the plateau.

Monday and Tuesday found only a small group,
chiefly volunteers, continuing the hunt. As it turned
out, of course, Donn, after the first night, was never
within ten miles of those who were looking for him.
Losing his sense of direction in the mist, he had gone
down off the mountain on the north side, into a region
seldom explored. The only trail which runs through
it is very obscure, overgrown and poorly marked.
Known as the North Peak's Trail, it runs almost
directly north until it reaches one of the little streams
that help to form the head-waters of the Wassataquoik
(pronounced, *Wa-see-tah-cook*) River.

AFTERWORD

The rivulet Donn followed, eventually led him to the main stream, and he paralleled that until he crossed over to the East Branch of the Penobscot River, on the opposite shore of which is the McMoarn Camp.

Even when Donn reached the camp, known in the Maine woods as "Lunksoos," he was far from any *real* civilization. The easiest approach to "Lunksoos" is by way of the East Branch of the Penobscot River itself, the nearest civilization being fourteen miles down the river, at Grindstone. The village of Stacyville is eight miles away, but can be reached only over a tote road which is in bad condition and must be traversed on foot.

As soon as Donn was safe in the McMoarn cabin, Mr. McMoarn notified the telephone operator that the boy had been found and the good news was rapidly spread. Three hours later, or about four o'clock in the afternoon, Dr. Ernest T. Young, accompanied by Chief of Police Picard of Millinocket, arrived at "Lunksoos" to look after Donn. A few hours later, the boy's two uncles, Dr. Arthur C. Ryan and Harold Fendler, arrived after a trip on foot from Stacyville along the old tote road.

The next morning, Donn was carried down to the shore of the river, where a canoe awaited him. Meanwhile, Mrs. Fendler had reached Grindstone, fourteen miles away.

AFTERWORD

In the course of the journey down to Grindstone, the river runs quite rapidly and is very shallow in spots. Huge boulders, some of them completely hidden, are abundant in the stream bed. Here, only expert and experienced hands prevented a river "spill" from being added to Donn's record of adventures. But, while racing through white water, Donn merely looked on, as any interested spectator would. It was just another example, in his eyes, of what may happen in the wilderness—and he seemed ready to meet any mishap with the same courage he had shown during those nine days in the forest.

Anxious to see her son again, as soon as possible, Mrs. Fendler—accompanied by her loyal friend, Mrs. Charles Mangan, who had been constantly at her side throughout the long, soul-trying ordeal—had set out by canoe from Grindstone. The touching reunion between mother and son took place in mid-river, when the canoes met, about a quarter of a mile above Grindstone.

The party then continued down to the little Maine village where an ambulance waited to take Donn and his mother to Bangor. Mr. Fendler was confined at the Eastern Maine General Hospital, with a serious eye injury sustained in the course of the long hunt. And it was there, in a hospital room, that the reunion of the entire family took place.

Meanwhile, throughout the nine days that the boy was lost, millions of people followed the fruitless progress of the search in the press of the country. Although the searchers themselves had given up all thought of finding the boy alive, thousands of mothers throughout America still hoped for his safe return. Their spirit and their hope is perhaps best described in the concluding paragraphs of an editorial appearing in the Boston *Transcript* of July 27, 1939:

"But after the searchers had turned back, and after the press had pronounced his return hopeless, thousands of mothers in America did not give up hope. They scanned the papers daily for word; they watched their own sons a bit more closely. There was a stout trail of hope being blazed for this boy.

"And, if there was such amazing strength of survival in Donn, we wonder if it was not in large measure due to the powerful sending and receiving apparatus of mother-to-son and son-to-mother. For at no time in human life will men find a greater courage in their hearts and in their weary bodies than when in youth, like Donn, they are returning home."